MW01623819

LONO
and the
Magical Land Beneath the Sea
Adapted & illustrated by Caren Loebel-Fried
from
Mary Kawena Pukui's translation of "Moolelo Kahiko no Kumuhonua"
held in the Bishop Museum Archives

Kamahoi Press is an imprint of the Bishop Museum Press.

Bishop Museum Press
1525 Bernice Street
Honolulu, HI 96817
www.bishopmuseum.org/press

Native Hawaiian Culture and Arts Program

Ua lehulehu a manomano ka ʻikena a ka Hawaiʻi.
Great and numerous is the knowledge of the Hawaiians.
Ōlelo Noʻeau 2814

This project is funded under the Native Hawaiian Culture and Arts Program in celebration of the Legacy of Excellence of Native Hawaiian culture. The Legacy of Excellence volumes are devoted to generating an appreciation of Native Hawaiian traditions, art, and language through education, awareness, and recognition of excellence in Native Hawaiian achievement.

ISBN 1-58178-055-9

Book design by Nancy Watanabe

Printed in China

10 09 08 07 06 1 2 3 4 5

Library of Congress Cataloging-in-Publication Data

Loebel-Fried, Caren.

Lono and the magical land beneath the sea / by Caren Loebel-Fried.

p. cm.

Summary: Relates in bilingual text how Lono the fisherman discovers a magical world beneath the sea with wonderful plants that he brings back on land where they flourish to become the main foods of the Hawaiian islands.

ISBN 1-58178-055-9 (hardcover : alk. paper)
[1. Folklore--Hawaii. 2. Hawaiian language materials--Bilingual.] I. Title.

PZ90 .H27L64 2006
398.209969--dc22

2006023435

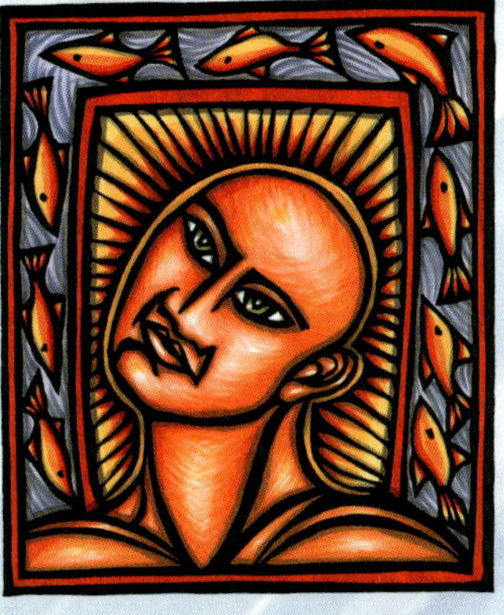

PULE HOOMAU

E Lono, alana mai Kahiki,
He pule ku keia ia oe e Lono.
E Lono lau ai nui,
E ua mai ka lani pili
Ka ua houlu ai,
Ka ua houlu kapa.
Popo kapa wai lehua
A Lono i ka lani.
E Lono e, kuua mai koko ai, koko ua.
Ulua mai.
Houlu ia mai ka ai, e Lono!
Houlu ia mai ka ia, e Lono!
Ka moomoo, kiheaheapalaa e Lono!
Amama. Ua noa.

O Lono, gift from Tahiti,
A prayer direct to you, O Lono.
O Lono of the broad leaf,
Let the low-hanging cloud pour out its rain
To make the crops flourish,
Rain to make the *tapa* plant flourish.
Wring out the dark rain clouds
Of Lono in the heavens.
O Lono, shake out a net full of food, a net full of rain.
Gather them together for us.
Accumulate food, O Lono!
Collect fish, O Lono!
Wauke shoots and the coloring matter for *tapa*, O Lono!
Amen. It is free.

CHANT FROM MALO, *HAWAIIAN ANTIQUITIES*, 1951.

Long ago, before many people inhabited this land, a fisherman named Lono lived in Keauhou on the island of Hawai'i. Most days were sunny and warm, and Lono could always smell the sea in the fresh breezes. When he wasn't fishing, Lono spent his days carving fishhooks and weaving basket traps.

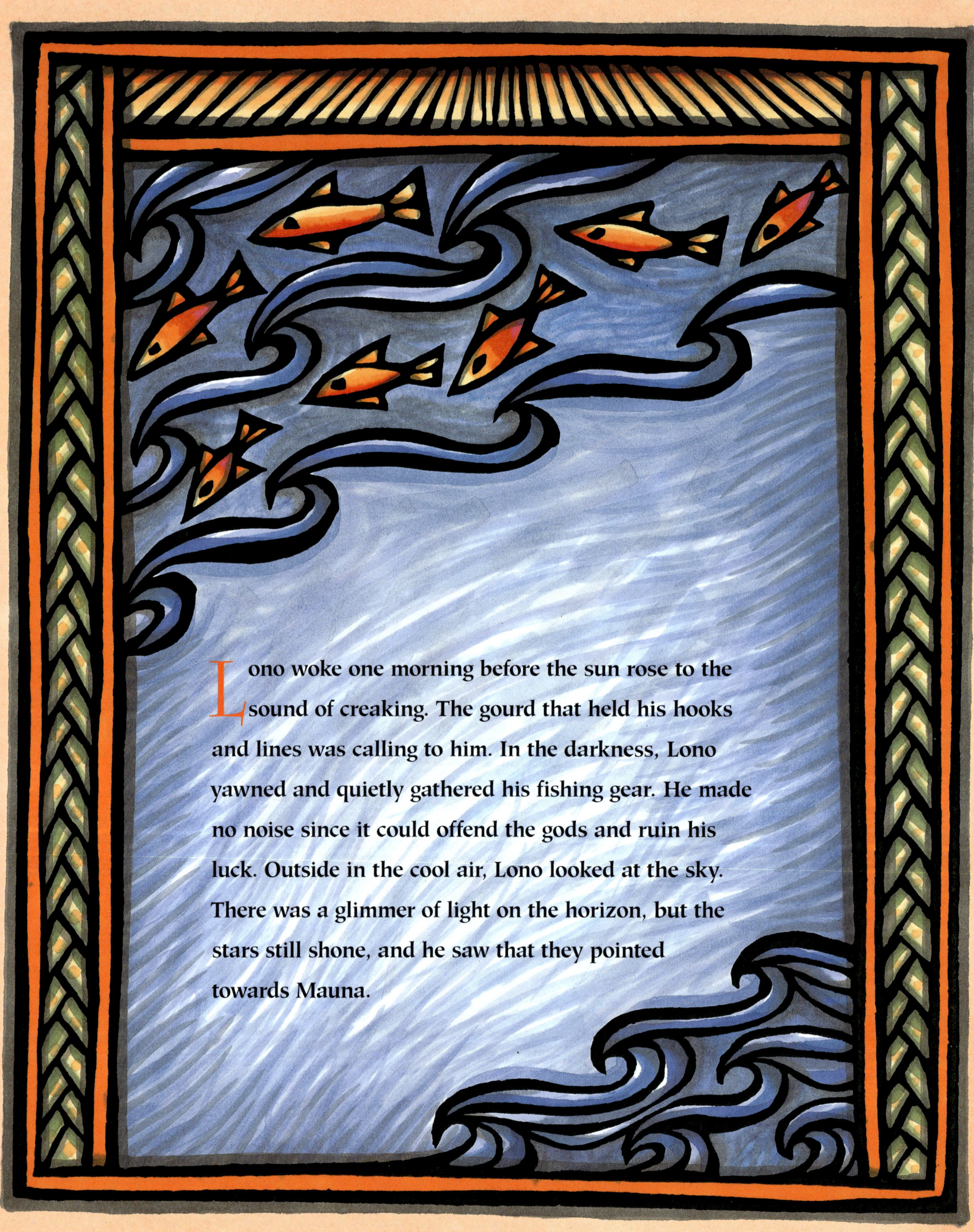

Lono woke one morning before the sun rose to the sound of creaking. The gourd that held his hooks and lines was calling to him. In the darkness, Lono yawned and quietly gathered his fishing gear. He made no noise since it could offend the gods and ruin his luck. Outside in the cool air, Lono looked at the sky. There was a glimmer of light on the horizon, but the stars still shone, and he saw that they pointed towards Mauna.

So Lono walked to Mauna, his favorite fishing grounds. After placing a small offering on the altar for the god of fishing, he pulled his canoe to the water, put his gear inside, and paddled just past the reef.

Lono tied a pebble to a baited hook and cast the line into the water. It sank down. After a few minutes, he felt a tug and quickly pulled the line in. He found that the tip of his fishhook had broken off. Thinking it must have gotten caught on the coral, Lono tied another hook onto the line and cast it again, away from the reef. After a minute, he felt a tug, but when he pulled the line in, he found that fishhook had broken, too. Lono sighed. These hooks took a long time to carve.

He tried a third hook, but that hook came back broken, too.

Lono dove into the sea

to investigate.

Beneath the sea, at the foundation of the earth, Lono discovered a magical land filled with wonderful plants that he had never before seen. A great man who looked like a god stood in the middle of the greenery with a young woman beside him. The man spoke. "I am Kumuhonua and this is my daughter, Hina-kauo. Lono, we welcome you to Kanuupapa." Lono saw in the young woman's hand the broken ends of his fishhooks.

** The name Kumuhonua means "foundation of the earth."*

There were many food plants growing there that were new to Lono. Everywhere he looked, a different plant interested him, with leaves of many shapes, sizes, and colors waving gently to him, and heavy fruit hanging here and there. Kumuhonua said, "Stay for a while, here in the land beneath the sea, to eat these plants and learn how to grow them." Lono smiled at Kumuhonua and nodded. "I will stay," he said.

Kalo

Kumuhonua taught Lono about taro. "*Kalo* likes to grow in wet places," he said. "It grows well in lower land areas but also higher up the mountains, as long as it has plenty of water. After nine to eighteen months, when the *kalo* plant is fully grown, it is ready to be pulled out of the ground. The baby plants growing out of the sides can be cut off and planted. The top part of the parent plant can also be cut off and replanted, and a new *kalo* plant will grow. The stems and young leaves can be cooked and eaten, and the corm can be steamed and pounded into a nutritious paste called *poi*. The juice from the *kalo* is used to reduce fevers, and the stem leaf is rubbed on insect bites to prevent swelling and pain."

`uala

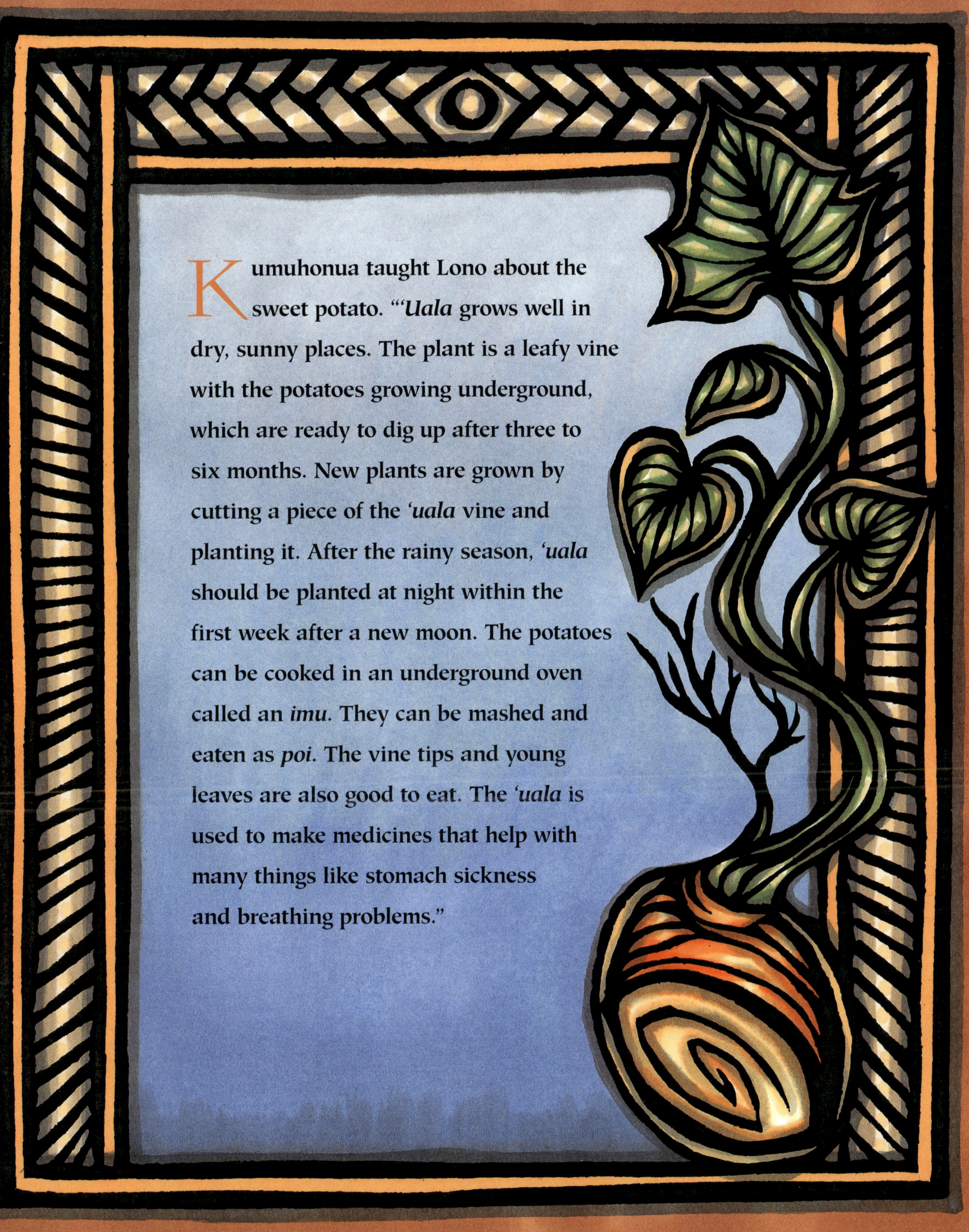

Kumuhonua taught Lono about the sweet potato. "'*Uala* grows well in dry, sunny places. The plant is a leafy vine with the potatoes growing underground, which are ready to dig up after three to six months. New plants are grown by cutting a piece of the *'uala* vine and planting it. After the rainy season, *'uala* should be planted at night within the first week after a new moon. The potatoes can be cooked in an underground oven called an *imu*. They can be mashed and eaten as *poi*. The vine tips and young leaves are also good to eat. The *'uala* is used to make medicines that help with many things like stomach sickness and breathing problems."

Kō

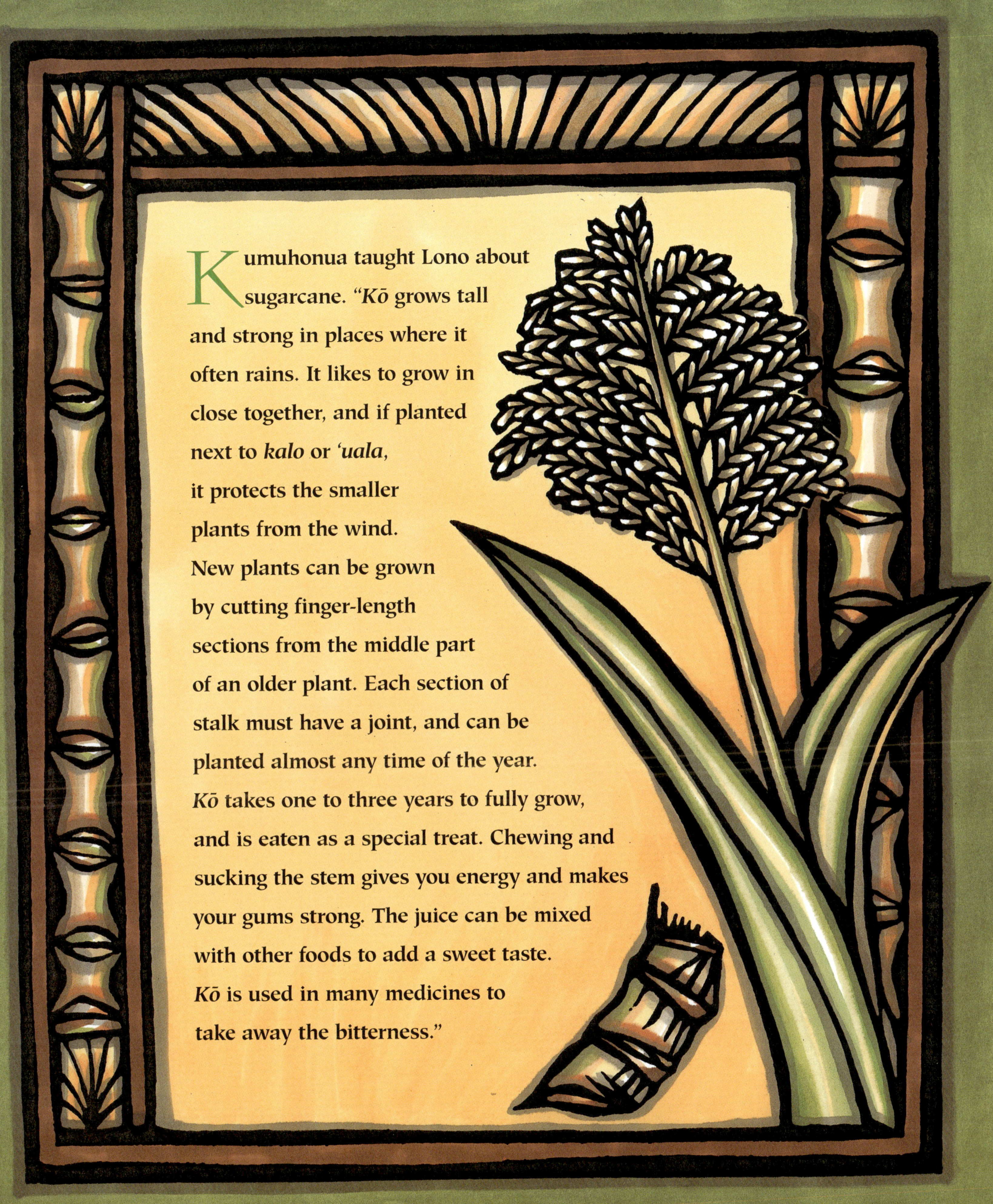

Kumuhonua taught Lono about sugarcane. "*Kō* grows tall and strong in places where it often rains. It likes to grow in close together, and if planted next to *kalo* or *'uala*, it protects the smaller plants from the wind. New plants can be grown by cutting finger-length sections from the middle part of an older plant. Each section of stalk must have a joint, and can be planted almost any time of the year. *Kō* takes one to three years to fully grow, and is eaten as a special treat. Chewing and sucking the stem gives you energy and makes your gums strong. The juice can be mixed with other foods to add a sweet taste. *Kō* is used in many medicines to take away the bitterness."

maiá

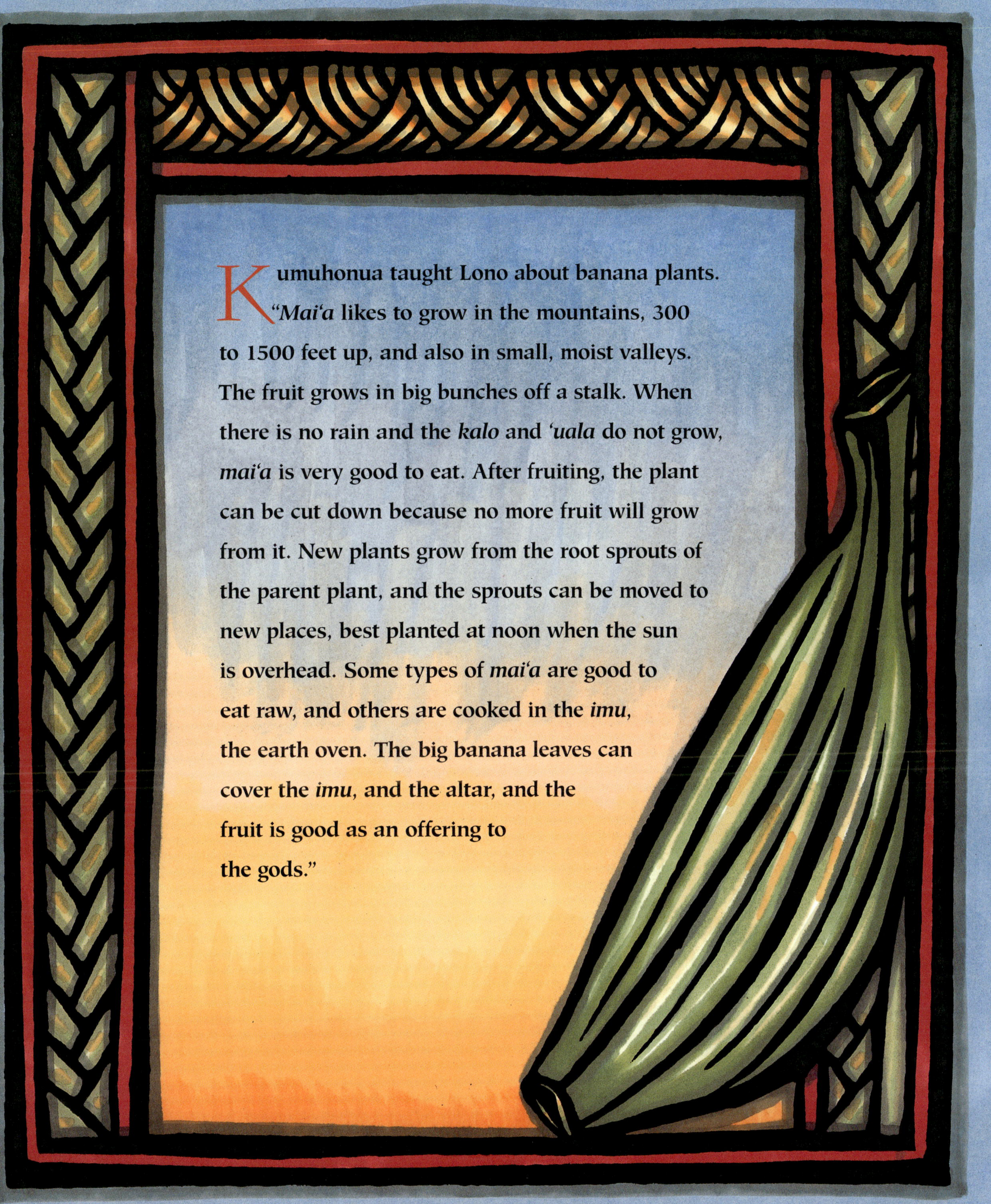

Kumuhonua taught Lono about banana plants. "*Mai'a* likes to grow in the mountains, 300 to 1500 feet up, and also in small, moist valleys. The fruit grows in big bunches off a stalk. When there is no rain and the *kalo* and *'uala* do not grow, *mai'a* is very good to eat. After fruiting, the plant can be cut down because no more fruit will grow from it. New plants grow from the root sprouts of the parent plant, and the sprouts can be moved to new places, best planted at noon when the sun is overhead. Some types of *mai'a* are good to eat raw, and others are cooked in the *imu*, the earth oven. The big banana leaves can cover the *imu*, and the altar, and the fruit is good as an offering to the gods."

ʻawa

Kumuhonua taught Lono about kava. "'*Awa* grows well in places where it rains all the time, along shady stream banks and in forest ranges where trees protect it from the sun. New plants can grow from sections of the stem laid along the ground to root. It takes the *'awa* plant two to three years to mature, but the plant can live for a very long time and be passed down to your children, and then to their children. A ceremonial drink is made by chewing the root and mixing it with water. The relaxing drink is also enjoyed by people after a long day of working. The *'awa* roots can be an offering to the gods, and parts of the plant can be used as a medicine for headaches and to help you sleep."

After one month had passed, it was time for Lono to return to his home in Keauhou. Kumuhonua and Hina-kauo gathered the tops of taro corms, cuttings from a sweet potato vine, the middle sections of sugarcane stalks, root sprouts from banana plants, and joints from an *'awa* shrub, and gave these to Lono. Lono thanked Kumuhonua and Hina-kauo and held tightly onto the plantings as he swam back up to the surface of the sea.

Lono followed all of Kumuhonua's instructions. He planted *kalo* in marshy lowlands, on stream banks, and also in moist upland areas. He planted *'uala* cuttings in dry areas, in the lowlands, and also high up on the mountain slopes.

Lono planted *kō* at Kauhakō and Ka'awaloa, and in areas where rain often falls. He planted *mai'a* in gulches and in moist areas up in the mountains. He planted *'awa* throughout Kona and in moist valleys where the sun was not too strong.

The plants grew well. The days and years passed and soon other people learned how to grow these plants themselves. They made more plants from the old plants, and soon the plants grew all over the islands of Hawai'i, feeding many families. Generation after generation, the people of Hawai'i flourished, just like the plants that Lono brought from the magical land beneath the sea.

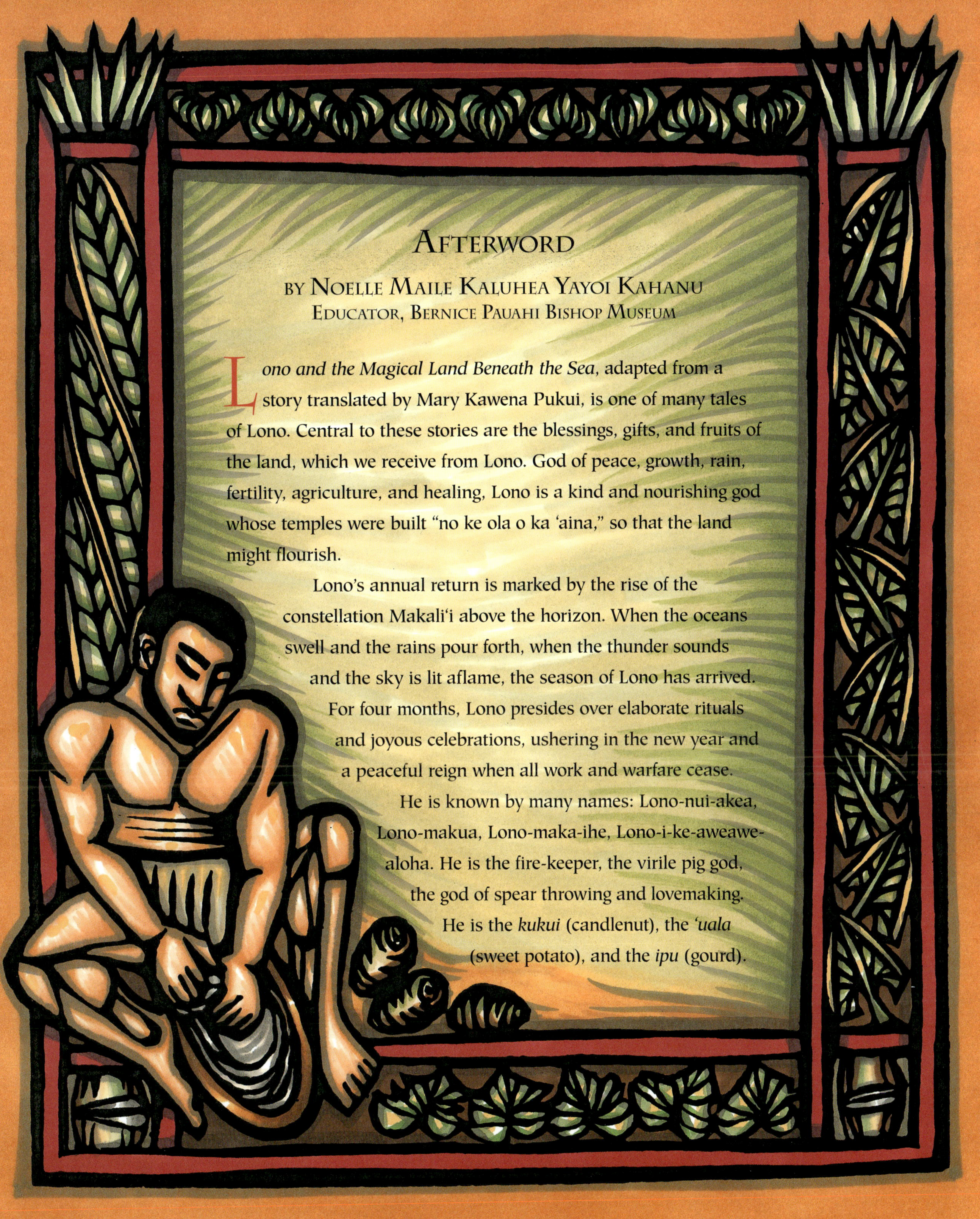

Afterword

by Noelle Maile Kaluhea Yayoi Kahanu
Educator, Bernice Pauahi Bishop Museum

L*ono and the Magical Land Beneath the Sea*, adapted from a story translated by Mary Kawena Pukui, is one of many tales of Lono. Central to these stories are the blessings, gifts, and fruits of the land, which we receive from Lono. God of peace, growth, rain, fertility, agriculture, and healing, Lono is a kind and nourishing god whose temples were built "no ke ola o ka 'aina," so that the land might flourish.

Lono's annual return is marked by the rise of the constellation Makali'i above the horizon. When the oceans swell and the rains pour forth, when the thunder sounds and the sky is lit aflame, the season of Lono has arrived. For four months, Lono presides over elaborate rituals and joyous celebrations, ushering in the new year and a peaceful reign when all work and warfare cease.

He is known by many names: Lono-nui-akea, Lono-makua, Lono-maka-ihe, Lono-i-ke-aweawe-aloha. He is the fire-keeper, the virile pig god, the god of spear throwing and lovemaking. He is the *kukui* (candlenut), the *'uala* (sweet potato), and the *ipu* (gourd).

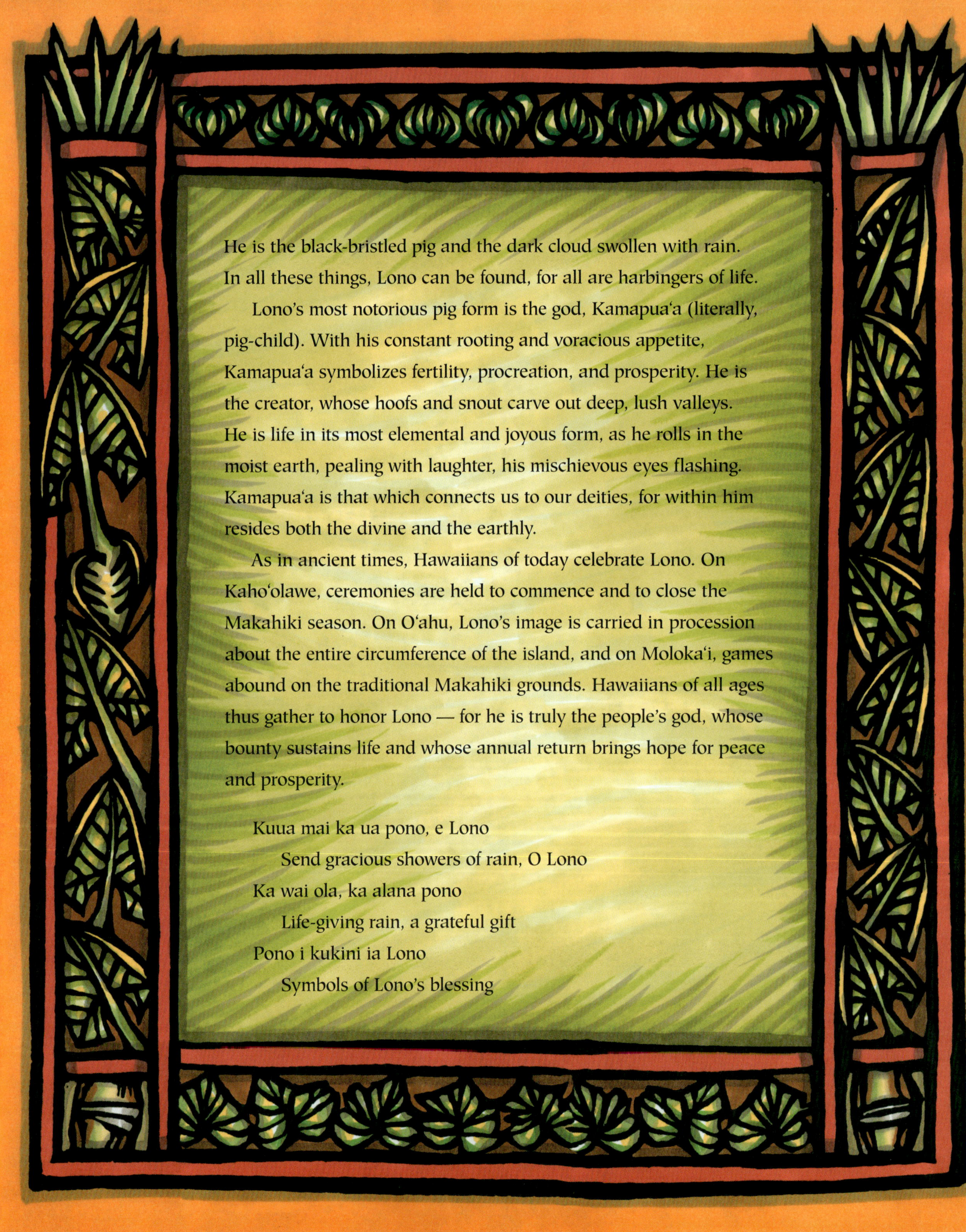

He is the black-bristled pig and the dark cloud swollen with rain. In all these things, Lono can be found, for all are harbingers of life.

Lono's most notorious pig form is the god, Kamapua'a (literally, pig-child). With his constant rooting and voracious appetite, Kamapuaʻa symbolizes fertility, procreation, and prosperity. He is the creator, whose hoofs and snout carve out deep, lush valleys. He is life in its most elemental and joyous form, as he rolls in the moist earth, pealing with laughter, his mischievous eyes flashing. Kamapuaʻa is that which connects us to our deities, for within him resides both the divine and the earthly.

As in ancient times, Hawaiians of today celebrate Lono. On Kahoʻolawe, ceremonies are held to commence and to close the Makahiki season. On Oʻahu, Lono's image is carried in procession about the entire circumference of the island, and on Molokaʻi, games abound on the traditional Makahiki grounds. Hawaiians of all ages thus gather to honor Lono — for he is truly the people's god, whose bounty sustains life and whose annual return brings hope for peace and prosperity.

Kuua mai ka ua pono, e Lono
    Send gracious showers of rain, O Lono
Ka wai ola, ka alana pono
    Life-giving rain, a grateful gift
Pono i kukini ia Lono
    Symbols of Lono's blessing

Below is the original Hawaiian language version of this legend, from the Bishop Museum Archives in Honolulu, Hawai'i.

Moolelo Kahiko no Kumuhonua

Ma ka hanauna mua o Kumuhonua, oia ka mea mamua o ka hanauna akua a kanaka paha, mamua o ka honua i ka wa kahiko, aole i ikea na kanaka ma ka aina ia manawa kahiko. Nana mai ka ai a loaa i kekahi kanaka ano akua i kapa ia o Lono ka inoa. O Lono he kanaka lawai'a ia ma Kona, ua noho ia ma Keauhou Kona Akau. He hana pai kana. Mahope iho oia mau la ana i hana ai i ka lawai'a moana. Aia kekahi ko'a lawai'a ma Keauhou, o Mauna kona inoa, oia kahi e lawaia ai. Pau na makau i ka mokumoku. Minamina oia me kona kuhihewa he mau ma ke ko'a a lekei ke kanaka ma lalo e nana. Ua hoopaa ia e ka wahine o Hina-kauo, ke kaikamahine a Kumuhonua. I aku la o Lono i kekahi kanaka, "E noho oe i ka waa o kaua." Luu aku la ia a loaa ua wahine nei malalo. He aina ia a noho oia malaila. Ike oia i na mea hou, aole i ike mua, aka i ka ai ana a ike keia makemake i na mea ai, he uala, he kalo, he maia, he ko, he awa. Noho pu oia me laua malaila hookahi mahina a mahope malama oia ia mau mea a pau i mea kanu nana. Lawe mai la ia he kalo, he uala, he ko, he maia, he awa, a mahope ninau oia ka wa a me ka po i na mea e ku ai ke kanu i ka uala. He uala maka, kalo maka, pohuli maia, puna ko maka, uhi, me ka awa ka mea e ulu ai. Oia ka mea i ha'i ia mai iaia. E lawe i mea kanu nana a lawe mai la oia i na mea

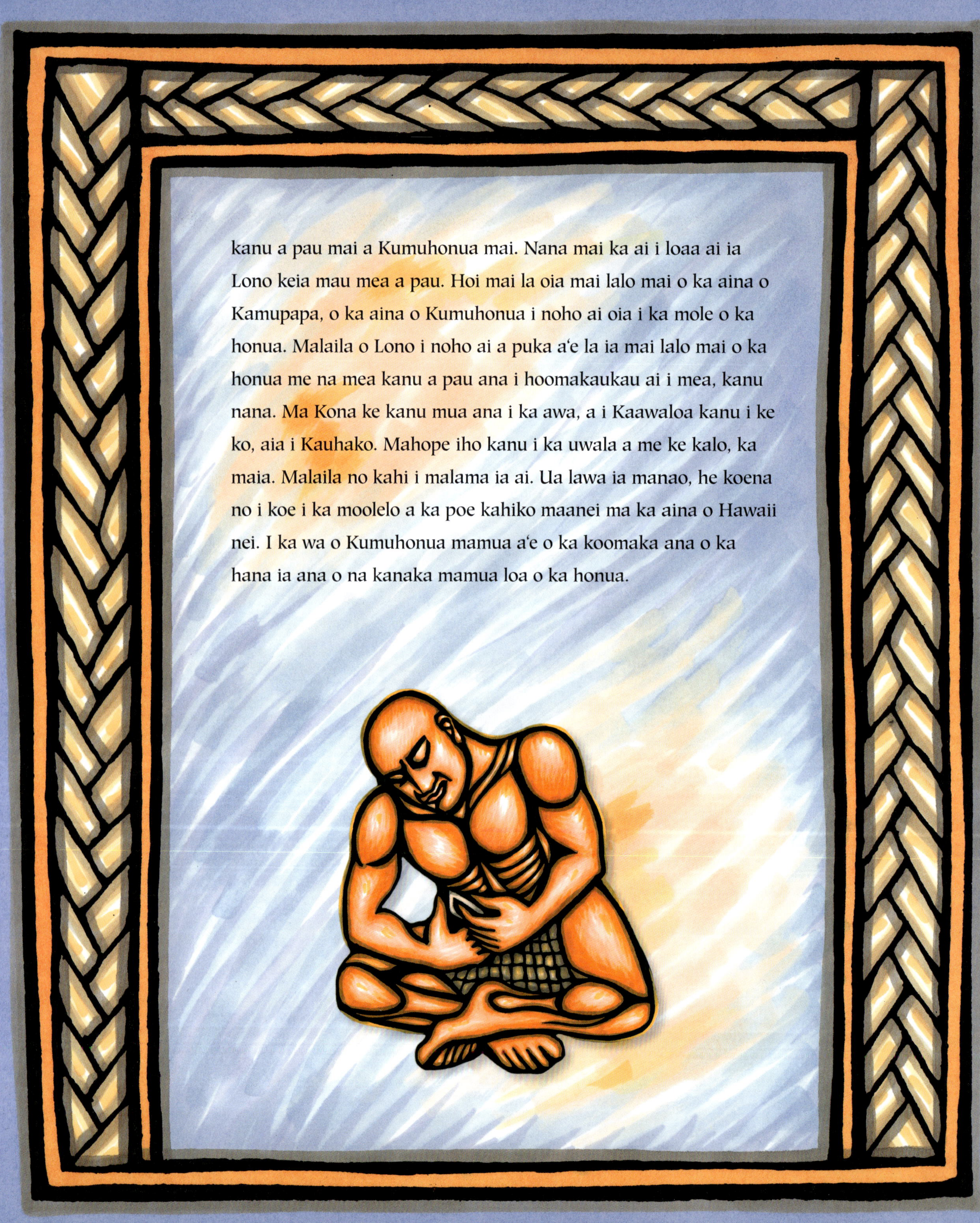

kanu a pau mai a Kumuhonua mai. Nana mai ka ai i loaa ai ia Lono keia mau mea a pau. Hoi mai la oia mai lalo mai o ka aina o Kamupapa, o ka aina o Kumuhonua i noho ai oia i ka mole o ka honua. Malaila o Lono i noho ai a puka aʻe la ia mai lalo mai o ka honua me na mea kanu a pau ana i hoomakaukau ai i mea, kanu nana. Ma Kona ke kanu mua ana i ka awa, a i Kaawaloa kanu i ke ko, aia i Kauhako. Mahope iho kanu i ka uwala a me ke kalo, ka maia. Malaila no kahi i malama ia ai. Ua lawa ia manao, he koena no i koe i ka moolelo a ka poe kahiko maanei ma ka aina o Hawaii nei. I ka wa o Kumuhonua mamua aʻe o ka koomaka ana o ka hana ia ana o na kanaka mamua loa o ka honua.

Sources

Abbott, Isabella Aiona. 1992. *Lā'au Hawai'i: Traditional Hawaiian Uses of Plants*. Honolulu: Bishop Museum Press.

Beckwith, Martha. 1970. *Hawaiian Mythology*. Honolulu: University of Hawai'i Press.

Handy, E.S. Craighill, Elisabeth G. Handy, & Mary Kawena Pukui. 1972. *Native Planters in Old Hawaii: Their Life, Lore, and Environment*. Honolulu: Bishop Museum Press.

Kahā'ulelio, Daniel. 2006. *Ka 'Oihana Lawai'a: Hawaiian Fishing Traditions*. Honolulu: Bishop Museum Press.

Kamakau, Samuel M. 1976. *Na Hana a ka Po'e Kahiko: The Works of the People of Old*. Honolulu: Bishop Museum Press.

Malo, David. 1951. *Hawaiian Antiquities: Mo'olelo Hawai'i*. Honolulu: Bishop Museum Press.

"Moolelo Kahiko no Kumuhonua, An Old Legend of Kumuhonua." Translated by Mary Pukui, Hawaiian Ethnographical Notes II, pp 234-237, Bishop Museum Library Archives, Honolulu. No date.

Te Rangi Hiroa (Peter H. Buck). 1957. *Arts and Crafts of Hawaii*. Honolulu: Bishop Museum Press.

Titcomb, Margaret. 1972. *Native Use of Fish in Hawaii*. Honolulu: University of Hawai'i Press.

About the Art

The art in this book is made with hand-colored block prints. The technique is similar to Hawaiian *'ohe kapala* which was practiced by highly skilled women. They decorated their kapa fabric with stamps carved from bamboo that were dipped in natural dyes and pressed into the cloth in geometric patterns. The prints in this book are made from linoleum and rubber blocks, printed with black ink, and then painted with washes of colored inks.